Night of Mysterious Blessings

Sally Metzger

illustrated by
Courtney Smith

ELK LAKE PUBLISHING INC

PUBLISHING THE POSITIVE
Plymouth, Massachusetts

A Christian Company
ElkLakePublishingInc.com

Cover and Interior Design: Courtney Smith, Derinda Babcock
Editor(s): Derinda Babcock, Deb Haggerty
Illustrations: Courtney Smith

PUBLISHED BY: Elk Lake Publishing, Inc., 35 Dogwood Drive, Plymouth, MA 02360, 2021

_____

Library Cataloging Data
Names: Metzger, Sally (Sally Metzger)
Night of Mysterious Blessings / Sally Metzger
40 p. 21.6 cm × 21.6 cm (8. 5 in × 8. 5 in.)
Identifiers: ISBN-13: 978-1-64949-441-2 (paperback) | 978-1-64949-442-9 (hardcover) | 978-1-64949-443-6 (trade paperback) | 978-1-64949-444-3 (e-book)
Key Words: Stories in Verse; Christian; Bedtime & Dreams;; Sandman; Blessings; Values & Virtues; Children ages 5-8. Read along story
Library of Congress Control Number: 2021949762 Fiction

The night was so quiet.
I tried counting sheep.
My sheep were exhausted in
heaps, fast asleep.

Old Paws wouldn't budge—
not a growl or a bark.
I struggled to slumber
alone in the dark.

3

How long would I lie there?
I flipped and I flopped.
Uncovered and covered.
My thoughts never stopped.

My problems were bigger
than me that sad night.
I needed a friend.
I just didn't feel right.

I'd heard an odd tale
of some magical sand
That helps you to dream
right away like you planned.

Some fairytale guy
has a healthy supply,
Which calms you to sleep
like a sweet lullaby.

My curtains then danced
with the salty sea air.
The moon lit my doorway.
Was somebody there?

I blinked, then I saw him,
his eyes all a twinkle.
"I brought you some sand.
Would you care for a sprinkle?"

The Sandman seemed kind,
and his grin was so broad,
I thought, why not try?
And I gave him a nod.

"Magnificent child,
this night has you stressed,
Yet all that you need
is to know that you're blessed."

He smelled of the sea
and the breeze at the shore.
He chuckled so warmly
I hoped to hear more.

"Feel free to curl up–
you are safe in your bed.
Since God stays awake,
you have nothing to dread.

We all have our problems.
Relax.
Do your best,
Then leave things to God.
He'll take charge of the rest.

And God isn't somewhere
way up in the sky.
He's living inside you.
He hears every sigh.

With God in your heart,
you're incredibly strong!
God calls you his friend—
so you'll always belong.

While I'm just a guy
from a fairytale place,
Our God is as real
as the nose on your face.

This sand from the sea
can't compare to his care.
Now, breathe in his calm.
He's as near as the air."

My shoulders relaxed.
What I'd heard was so true.
No matter what happens,
God always comes through.

God's peace filled my heart,
so I smiled and I yawned.
I peeked only once,
and the Sandman was gone.

I opened my eyes
to a sunny new day.
My dream was the best,
but all dreams slip away.

I hoped to remember
that God is right here!
To share all my feelings,
to trust, and not fear.

I rolled on my side,
and I saw on the floor,
A trail of white sand
from my bed to the door!

I looked at Old Paws
as he stared at the mess.
He barked and he whined–
that's his way to confess.

28

Old Paws was a pup
when he last dug in sand.
That night on the beach,
he felt young—like God planned.

The sand's a reminder.
I treasure the stuff.
No matter my problems,
God's peace is enough!

The End ...

Or just the
beginning.

Discussion Questions

Let's call the boy in the story "Blessed,"
so we don't have to say "the boy in the story" all the time.

1. What do we mean by a "mystery?" Are there things that amaze you that you can't understand? What were some of the mysterious blessings that Blessed received? What do you think is the most wonderful thing he discovered during his fantastic night?

2. *Night of Mysterious Blessings* talks about God living in our hearts. Let's be very still, put our hands over our hearts, and say a prayer to God inside us. How do you feel knowing God is closer than the air you breathe? What color, size, or shape is your feeling? Do you believe your feeling is a blessing?

3. What blessing in your day or week wants to be told? During this week, we can go on a blessings hunt. Make a list of blessings each day. Share the list with a parent, grandparent, or someone special in your life. Ask them to please call you "Blessed" during the sharing.

4. How does finding a blessing make you feel inside? Would you like to keep hunting for blessings?

5. Blessed was sad, mad, and frustrated because he couldn't sleep. How did God bring good out of something bad?

32

6. Why was Blessed's heart necklace dear to him? What do you think the necklace meant? In the last picture of the book, we see light coming from Blessed's heart. Do you think the light has a special meaning? If so, what?

Crafts

1.   MY HEART'S HIS HOME NECKLACE   First, decorate a heart in any way you like. If you want, you can write words on the heart that want to be written. Then make a paper chain necklace and attach the heart to it. Let the necklace be a reminder—God is with you, for you, and inside you.

2.   BLESSINGS IN A JAR   Blessed treasured the mysterious sand, which he gathered and placed in a jar to remind him of the peace, love, and blessings he received that incredible night. Collect, draw, or build something that is a sign for you of God's love and blessings. Place your collection or creation in a jar and put your Blessings in a Jar somewhere you'll see it often. Let the jar remind you God is always with you, loving you just as you are.

About the Author

As a teacher, spiritual director, and retreat leader, Sally Metzger has nurtured the faith of youth for over twenty years. She treasures her role as confidant to young people finding their footing in God's world of grace. Sally has a Master of Theological Studies degree and developed and taught a course in faith formation for parents, religion teachers, and youth ministers. She is active in chaplain ministry and the author of the children's book *Jesus, Were You Little?* to be released in 2022. Sally cherishes family time and enjoys hiking, river rafting, and outdoor adventures.

About the Illustrator

Courtney Smith grew up in southwestern Colorado and later, attended college at Regis University, where she met and married a handsome rocket scientist. Together, they have welcomed five children and live in Franktown, Colorado. Courtney raises Great Pyrenees puppies, teaches CPR, travels internationally with USA Olympic wrestling hopefuls as an athletic trainer, and cheers on her children. In her free time, she loves to draw and sketch, creating images to enhance incredible stories.

Made in the USA
Middletown, DE
22 September 2022